About the Book

Cows are sacred in India, and it is a very fortunate family that can afford to buy one.

But Jaya doesn't feel lucky when he sees his family's new cow. Khubi is thin and ugly; not at all like the fat white cow Jaya pictured so vividly in his dreams and in his boasts to his schoolmate Shanti.

Khubi follows Jaya everywhere, getting him in trouble with his father and with his teacher. And each time Jaya tries to milk her, playful Khubi circles away from him, making the task impossible.

Tired of being punished because of the new cow, Jaya runs off to the bazaar—where real trouble awaits him.

How could Jaya guess that he'd be happy to see the scrawny cow among the gathering crowd or that Khubi's tricks would help save him?

Eva Grant's entertaining adventure and Michael Hampshire's handsome, realistic drawings combine to give young readers an unusual, close-up look at India's village life and customs.

Coward, McCann & Geoghegan
New York

A COW FOR JAYA

by EVA GRANT

Illustrated by Michael Hampshire

To *My* Beautiful Ones!
Steven
David
Richard
Andrea
Carol
and
Jon

Text copyright © 1973 by Eva Grant

Illustrations copyright © 1973 by Michael Hampshire

Published simultaneously in Canada by
Longman Canada Limited, Toronto.
SBN: GB-698-30484-5
SBN: TR-698-20232-5
Library of Congress Catalog Card Number: 72-85618

PRINTED IN THE UNITED STATES OF AMERICA

06209

CONTENTS

1. A Cow of His Own

On his way home from school,
Jaya stepped out of the way
of the big white cow.
In the mud-brick village in India
where Jaya lived,
cows were free to wander
where they liked.

People believed it was a sin
for anyone to hurt a cow.
Jaya knew his father
had been saving money
for a long time
so his family could have
a cow of its own.

Jaya's mouth watered
when he thought of all
the milk and butter and cheese
the cow would give them.

When Jaya entered his house,
he found his father
counting the rupees he was
saving to buy the cow.
The silvery coins
were piled in little heaps
on the cot of woven string
which served as a table
during the day.

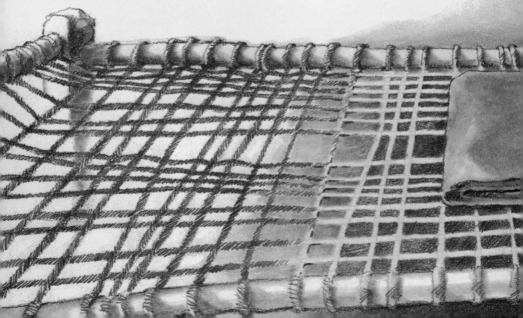

"Only about a hundred more,"
his father said, "and we will have
enough to buy a cow."
"Maybe it will not be
too long now,"
Jaya's mother said hopefully.

"How long?" asked Jaya.

"Very long," answered his mother,

"if you do nothing

but ask questions.

If we are ever to own a cow,

we all must work hard!"

2. "She's a Stupid Cow!"

At last one day,
when Jaya came home,
his father met him with good news.
"I found a man in the bazaar,"

he told Jaya,
"who had to sell his cow.
So I was able to buy her
for a low price.
Tomorrow we will have a cow."
Jaya's black eyes widened
like two round rupees.
"I can't wait to see her!"
he cried.
"May I stay home from school
and wait for her?"
"She will be waiting for you
when school is over,"
his father said.
"But remember, my son,
a cow is not a toy.

She will need care and attention.
We are counting on you to help."
Jaya hardly listened.

The next morning, in school,
he counted the moments
till closing time.
"Why are you so excited?"
whispered his friend, Shanti.
"You would be excited too,"
Jaya whispered back,
"if there was a beautiful fat cow
waiting for you at home!"
"A cow!" Shanti shook her head.
"I don't believe you!"
"A beautiful white cow!"
Jaya said once more.
"Come to my house
and see for yourself,
if you don't believe me!"

"Jaya!" The sound
of his teacher's voice
made him jump.
"You are not paying attention.
Is there something wrong?"
Jaya hung his head. "It's only
that we are getting a cow today."
"Well!" said his teacher.
"Then you may leave early.
It is not every day
that one gets a new cow."

Jaya raced home,
his bare feet
making the dust fly.

And there was a cow standing
in front of the hut.
But *this* could not be the new cow!

Instead of being fat
and big and white,
as he had pictured her,
this cow was small and skinny
and of no particular color.
Her worn rope collar
didn't add much to her looks.

"Out of my way, Ugly One!"
Jaya shouted.
But the cow didn't move.
Jaya's mother came to the door.
"This strange cow won't go away,"
Jaya complained.
"This strange cow is ours,"
his mother said.
"Her name is Khubi."
"Khubi!"
Khubi meant Beautiful One.
"How can you call
such a cow Khubi?"
Jaya wanted to know.
"All the same, her name is Khubi,"
his mother said quietly.

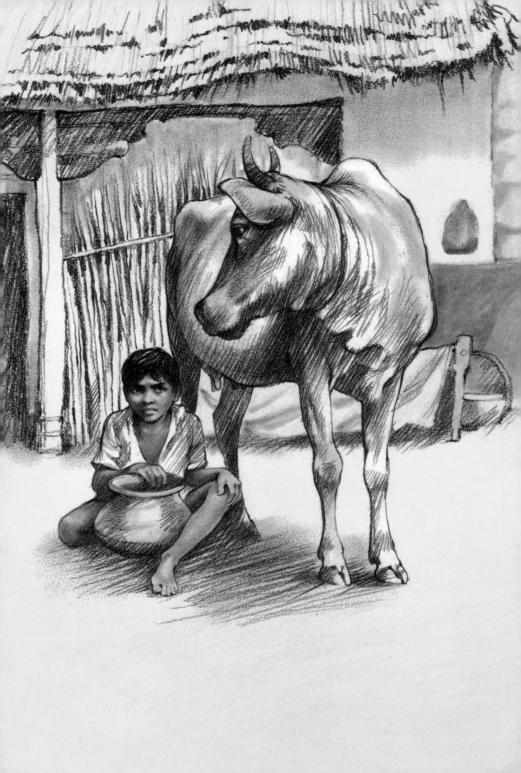

"You will have to learn to milk her."
Jaya had not known
how hard it was to milk a cow.
His father tried to teach him,
but Jaya was sure
he would never learn.
He got down beside Khubi
as he had seen his father do.
He grabbed the cow's udders
and pulled.
But more milk fell on the ground
than into the pail.
Khubi was no help.
She would not stand still.
How could he milk her
if she kept circling away from him?

He heard someone laughing
and looked up to see Shanti
holding her hand over her mouth.
"Clumsy!" she said.
"I came to see
your beautiful new cow.
I am thirsty for some milk."

Jaya's face burned.

"Even if her name is Khubi,"
he muttered,
"she is not a beautiful cow."
He glared into the almost empty pail.
"See, she doesn't even know
how to give milk.
She's a stupid cow!"

"Don't say such things
about your cow.
It is not right!"
Shanti looked fearfully about her
as if she were afraid something
terrible would happen to Jaya.

Every morning Jaya had to gather
fresh vegetables
for Khubi's breakfast.
"You are a pest,"
he said to her.
"Moo!" she answered back.

For if Jaya did not
like the new cow,
she loved him just the same.
Everywhere he turned,
there she was,
nuzzling him and shoving him.
"Why can't we tie her up?"
he asked his father.
"Would you tie up
a creature that gives us food?"
his father said in amazement.
Jaya did not answer.
But he was thinking hard.
If he led her into the jungle,
the cow would never find
her way home.

He sighed.

His father had saved so long
and worked so hard to buy this cow.

Jaya knew he could not harm
his father's cow.

But he was sure
he would never get to like Khubi.

3. At the Bazaar

One morning, trudging to school,
Jaya heard the clump-clump
of Khubi's footsteps behind him.
He picked up a stick
and waved it at her.
"Go home!" he yelled.
But Khubi, her eyes filled with love,
walked up to him.

"For shame!" said Shanti,
who was watching.
"Would you beat your own cow?"
she said in a horrified voice.
"She's not *my* cow!" Jaya exploded.
"She's my father's cow!
And besides, I never touched her."
He took hold of the cow's rope
and led her back to the house.

This made him late,
and he had to stay after school
for punishment.
He arrived home
too late to do his chores,
so his father made him stay
in the house for punishment.
And it was all Khubi's fault!
The next morning
there was no school.
When Jaya went outside,
Khubi was waiting for him.
Jaya said,
"You are a good-for-nothing cow.
You aren't even worth
the food you eat!"

Then he turned and ran off.
He would go to the bazaar,
where all the shopkeepers
set up their stalls,
to forget his troubles.

But Khubi loved the noise and color
of the city streets too.
If Jaya had looked back, he
would have seen her following him.
Soon Jaya left the country road.

When he arrived at the silk stalls,
he stopped to look around.
He picked up a piece of silk
in his hand to test its quality.
He liked to pretend
he was a rich shopkeeper.

"What do you want, boy?"
The owner of the silk stall
had come outside and
was looking right at Jaya.
"I need nothing right now,"
Jaya said.

"Then keep moving,"
said the shopkeeper.
Jaya left quickly.
Business must be bad today,
he thought.

He walked on.
Khubi still followed.
Once she stopped to sniff
the strange odors in the bazaar.
While Jaya watched
a snake charmer at work,
Khubi lowered her head
to search out a blade of grass.

Jaya's attention
was caught
by a stall hung
with hundreds
of fascinating things.
There was even
a leather collar
for a cow.
It was trimmed
with shiny brass bells.
Jaya reached
for a small bamboo flute.
He put it to his mouth to try it.
"Give me that!"
A strange boy

with a rough voice
pulled the flute from Jaya's hand.
Then the boy fled.

4. There Was Khubi

"Thieves! Catch them!"
the shopkeeper shouted.
Before he knew what
was happening, Jaya felt
a powerful hand grab him.
"I have caught a thief! Police!"
"No! No!" cried Jaya, terrified.
He tried to explain.
But the shopkeeper
never stopped yelling for a moment.

Jaya looked about him wildly.

There was Khubi!

With a desperate tug,

Jaya slipped

from the shopkeeper's grip.

He ran and hid behind Khubi.

The shopkeeper tried to grab Jaya,

but Khubi blocked his way.

When the shopkeeper tried

to reach around her,

Khubi circled in front of him.

Around and around she circled,

just as she had

when Jaya tried to milk her.

Around and around

chased the shopkeeper,

but Khubi was always there,
protecting Jaya.
A crowd had gathered.
"Will no one help me
catch this thief?"
the shopkeeper cried.

But no one would help him
pull Jaya away from Khubi.
What if they harmed the cow?
"He must be a good boy,"
said one of the onlookers
to his friend, "if his cow
watches over him like this."

Jaya, his heart pounding,
pressed close to Khubi.

He knew that if he tried
to run away, he would be
handed over to a policeman.
And here came one!
He was pushing before him
the very boy who had
escaped with the flute.

"Here is your thief,"
said the policeman.
"I am sorry,"
the shopkeeper said to Jaya,
"for the trouble I have caused you.
You may pick out anything you like."

Jaya looked longingly at the flute.
Then he looked
at Khubi's worn collar.
Khubi had saved him
from going to jail!
"I'll take that collar for my cow,"
he said. "The one with
the little brass bells."
The shopkeeper
handed him the collar,

thankful he had not picked out
something more costly.
But one of the bystanders,
a good customer, said,
"Why don't you let the boy
keep the flute?
It's the least you can do
after scaring him half to death!"
So the shopkeeper gave the flute
to Jaya.
Jaya fastened the new collar
around Khubi's neck.
"What a beautiful cow!"
he heard a man say.
"I wish I had enough rupees
to buy such a cow!"

5. My Beautiful One!

Jaya stared at Khubi,
who looked at him and mooed.
She still wasn't
the white cow he had dreamed of,
but with her shiny new collar
she *did* look handsome.
You are *my* Khubi, he thought.
My Beautiful One!

They started for home.
Jaya walked close to Khubi.
He was proud to walk beside
such a beautiful cow.
As they neared the village,
Jaya played a lively song
on his flute.

The sound of Khubi's bells
added to the fun.

Shanti heard them
and came running out
to see who was making the music.
"What a handsome pair!" said Shanti.
She wanted to know where
the collar and the flute came from.
Jaya said, "It's a long story.
Walk along with us
and I will tell you all about it."

"Well, it's time you arrived!"
Jaya's father greeted them
when they reached home.
"Maybe we ought to tie up
the cow and you too, Jaya!"
Jaya's black eyes danced.
"You wouldn't tie up
your only son and his only cow,
would you?"

His father laughed.
"Go feed your cow and milk her,
foolish one," he said.
"A boy who takes care of his cow
will never go hungry."

"Let me help," said Shanti.
"If you will feed her," Jaya said,
"I will play her a little song
on my flute.
Then maybe
she will let me milk her."
Khubi chewed the fresh greens
and listened to Jaya's music.
Jaya got down
and pressed his forehead
against the cow's warm flank.
With steady hands,
he pulled at the cow's udders.
Khubi stood quietly
while her rich milk
filled the pail.

Soon the pail was full.
Shanti looked at Jaya.

"I am thirsty," she said softly.
Jaya smiled up at her
and gave her some
warm, white milk.
Khubi shook her head.

The bells on her new collar
made many happy sounds.

About the Author

Reading, music and the theater are among EVA GRANT'S favorite recreations. She has also traveled extensively in Western Europe and Israel.

Mrs. Grant began taking writing courses at the New School for Social Research and later joined the Bank Street College Writer's Lab. Her stories and poems have been published in many magazines, including *The Instructor*.

Mrs. Grant and her husband, Reuben, make their home in South Orange, New Jersey. The Grants have two daughters, Arleen and Judith, and six grandchildren.

About the Artist

As a young boy MICHAEL HAMPSHIRE lived on the Yorkshire moors in England; he later studied art at Leeds University.

An enthusiastic amateur archaeologist, he has traveled widely to such places as Nepal, Ceylon, Africa and Central America. He brings to *A Cow for Jaya* the firsthand observations of a recent summer spent in India and has drawn on his trips to create vividly realistic foreign settings in the many books he has illustrated, including *Getting to Know the Suez Canal*.

Between travels, Mr. Hampshire lives in Greenwich Village in New York City.

About the Series

Boys and girls who are just beginning to read on their own will find the Break-of-Day books enjoyable and easy to read. Lively, fresh stories that are far ranging and varied in content combine with attractive illustrations. Large, clear type and simple language, but without vocabulary controls, keep the stories readable and fun.